DISNEY
MICKEY'S CHRISTMAS

STORYBOOK TREASURY

DISNEY PRESS

LOS ANGELES • NEW YORK

This book is a gift for:

_____

CONTENTS

"Christmas is a time for giving. A time to be with one's family."

—Bob Cratchit

MICKEY'S
CHRISTMAS CAROL

O

NE CHRISTMAS EVE long ago, a thick blanket of white covered the streets of London. Gently falling snow tickled the townsfolk hurrying home with their Christmas gifts.

But one person was not thinking about Christmas trees or presents. He paid no attention to the festively decorated houses.

His name was
Ebenezer Scrooge.

Scrooge hurried past a group of Christmas carolers.

"Penny for the poor?"

one of them called.

"Bah! Humbug!" Scrooge replied.

He wouldn't give a penny to anyone. If the poor wanted to be rich, they could work as hard as he did.

Inside Scrooge's office, his assistant, Bob Cratchit, was busy working.

"A-a-choo!" Cratchit sneezed.

It was bitterly cold, and even the ink for his quill had frozen. He didn't think Mr. Scrooge would mind if he used just one little piece of coal.

Cratchit carefully opened the furnace. He was just about to put in the piece of coal when the door swung open and

Scrooge burst in.

"What are you doing
with that piece of coal?"

he shouted at Cratchit.

"J-just trying to thaw out the ink," Cratchit stammered.
But Scrooge didn't care.
"You used a piece
last week," he said.

"Now get on
with your work,
Cratchit!"

While Cratchit went back to copying papers, old Scrooge sat down at his desk and lovingly polished his gold coins until they glowed.

Rubbing his hands together with glee, he weighed the coins on his scale and stacked them carefully on the desktop.

Suddenly, the door flew open with a bang.

"Merry Christmas!" Scrooge's nephew, Fred, shouted. "Merry Christmas, Uncle Scrooge!"

"Bah! Humbug!" Scrooge snorted.

"What's so merry about it? I'll tell you what Christmas is.

It's just another workday."

"But sir, Christmas is a time for giving. A time to be with one's family," Cratchit explained.

"I say, bah humbug!" Scrooge scowled.

Fred invited Scrooge to Christmas dinner, but Scrooge refused. And with that, Scrooge kicked his nephew out of the office.

A while later, Bob Cratchit looked
at the clock and stepped down from
his stool.

"It's two minutes fast,"
Scrooge snapped.

"Oh, never mind.
You may go."

"O-oh, thank you, sir," Cratchit stammered in
amazement.

"And I suppose you'll be wanting off tomorrow," Scrooge barked. "But be here all the earlier the next day."

"Thank you, Mr. Scrooge!" Cratchit cried. He snatched up Scrooge's bag of laundry and was gone in an instant, shouting "Merry Christmas" as he went.

Later, Scrooge locked up his office and hurried home through the swirling snow. Climbing his dark, steep steps, he took an old key from his pocket.

As he went to open the door, Scrooge took a closer look at his door knocker. He gasped! On the knocker was the face of his old business partner, Jacob Marley.

The face on the door began to move.

"Scrooooge!" it called softly.

Frightened, Scrooge yanked the door open and ran inside. He flew up the stairs three at a time. Behind him, he heard the sound of chains clanking.

Looking over his shoulder, Scrooge froze in his tracks. The ghost of Marley had come back to haunt him!

Scrooge ran into his bedroom and slammed the door. Quickly, he bolted every lock.

"That's it! No ghost can get through that!" he said.

But in the dark shadows of his bedroom, Scrooge shivered.

Clink . . . clink . . .
clink . . . clink . . .

The chains dragged closer and closer. Scrooge sank down in his chair, his teeth chattering in fear.

Soon enough, the ghost appeared before him. Chains circled his body. Attached to him were several large, heavy objects.

As Marley inched closer to Scrooge,
he tripped over Scrooge's cane.

The ghost went flying!

Scrooge trembled with fright as the ghost picked
himself up. "Scrooge, don't you recognize your
old business partner?" the ghost asked.
"It is I, Jacob Marley."

Scrooge took a
closer look at him.

"Marley!
It *is* you."

The ghost held up his chains. "Ebenezer, remember how when I was alive, I would rob the widows and swindle the poor? I was wrong. And as punishment, I'm forced to carry around these heavy chains through eternity. I'm doomed, and the same thing will happen to you, Ebenezer Scrooge."

"No, it can't! It mustn't!" Scrooge cried.

"Tonight, you will be visited by three spirits," Marley continued. "Listen to them. Do what they say. Or your chains will be heavier than mine. Farewell, Ebenezer, farewell."

And with another clanking of his chains, Marley was gone.

Scrooge quickly pulled on his nightshirt and cap, hopped into bed, and pulled the covers right up to his nose.

He was almost asleep

when a little figure with a top hat on his head and an umbrella in one hand stepped out of the shadows.

"I am the Ghost of Christmas Past,"

he told Scrooge.

"You must come with me. There is not a moment to lose."

But Scrooge just laughed at the Spirit. "Look how small you are," he said. "You do not scare me. Go away!"

"Silence!" ordered the Spirit. "If men were measured by their kindness, you would be smaller than a grain of sand!"

"Catch hold of my coattails," the Spirit commanded. "We are going back to a time when Christmas was not a humbug!"

Scrooge hesitated, but remembering Marley's terrible warning, he grasped the Spirit and held on tightly.

The windows flew open, and instantly Scrooge and the Ghost of Christmas Past were soaring over rooftops and chimneys, the Spirit's little umbrella keeping them aloft.

Soon they came to a stop
outside a brightly lit house.
The Spirit set them both down
in the freshly fallen snow. Joyful
Christmas music drifted through
the air.

Peering through the windows, Scrooge couldn't believe his eyes. "Why, it's Isabelle!" he cried, suddenly remembering the girl he'd once loved. "But who is that she's dancing with so merrily?"

"That man was you, Scrooge,"

the Spirit whispered,

"in the days when you, too, were kind and cheerful." They watched a moment longer, and then the Spirit whisked Scrooge away to another scene.

Scrooge and the Spirit peered through another window. Inside, the Scrooge of many years before sat behind a desk covered in money. Isabelle stood in front of him, tears in her eyes.

"Is this my office?" Scrooge asked.

"Why is Isabelle crying?"

The Spirit gave Scrooge a withering look, and suddenly Scrooge remembered. He had taken Isabelle's home from her when she could not pay her bills, and had refused to marry her.

The Spirit turned from the window. "Your greed drove her away, Ebenezer. You were to marry her, but you loved only your money. And you lost her forever."

"No . . ." Scrooge moaned softly. "I loved Isabelle. Please, I cannot bear these memories. Take me home!"

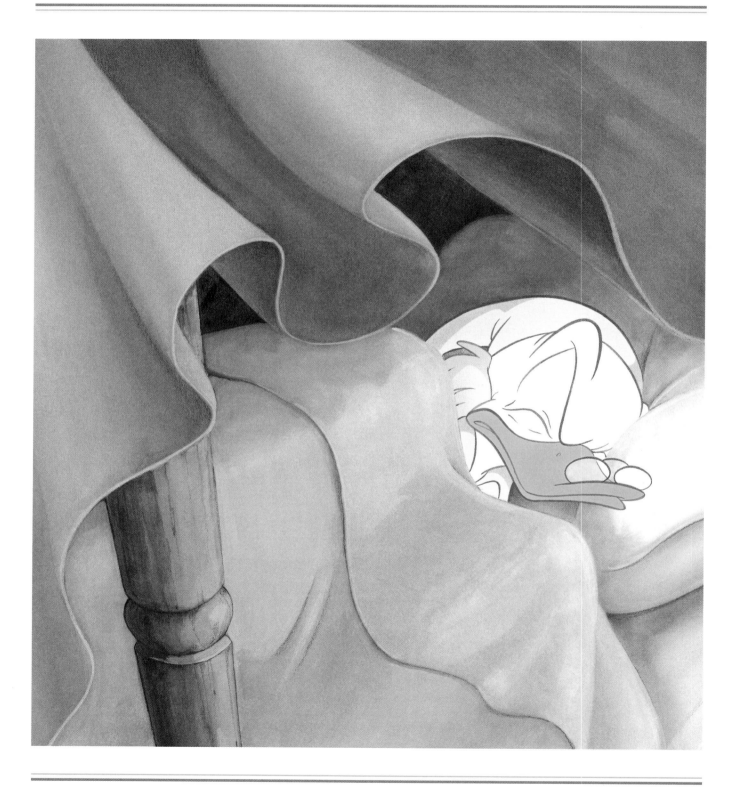

Suddenly, Scrooge found himself once more in his bed.

"That couldn't have happened,"

he said.

"I couldn't have flown through the air. That was just a bad dream."

Then he thought of Isabelle, and how his love of money had ruined his chance for happiness with her. Scrooge put his head down and sobbed into his pillow.

As he cried, Scrooge suddenly felt a heavy hand on his shoulder. Scrooge raised his head and found a fierce-looking giant feasting beside his bed.

"I am the Ghost of Christmas Present,"
boomed the giant.

"Oh, please," cried Scrooge. "Spare me!"

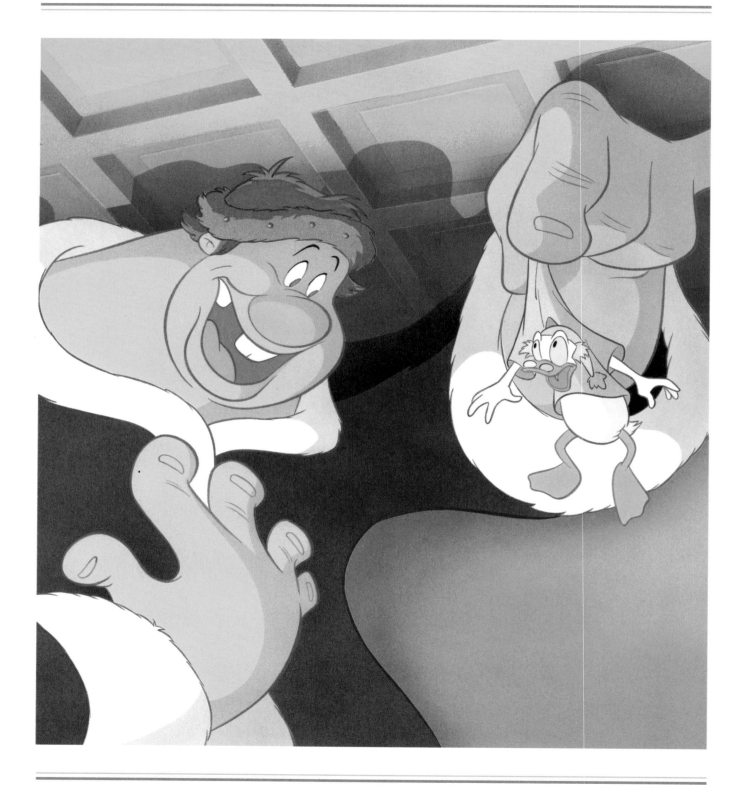

The giant picked up Scrooge by his nightshirt and examined him closely.

"No! Don't hurt me, please! Have mercy. Take my treasure. You can have it all," Scrooge cried.

"Keep your treasure, Scrooge," the Spirit replied. "It is of no use to me. Money cannot buy happiness, and only my generosity can save you now."

"Have a grape, won't you?" the Spirit told Scrooge, dropping him down into the middle of his feast. Slipping and sliding, Scrooge called out for help, but the Spirit just laughed.

"I have the power to give you life, but what have you ever given?" the Spirit asked Scrooge.

"Let us take a look."

"There's no time to lose," the Spirit cried, scooping up Scrooge and putting him in his pocket. He pushed open the roof and stepped outside, as though from a doll's house.

Scrooge peeked out of the giant's pocket.

"I wonder where we're going,"

he said to himself.

Pulling Scrooge from his pocket, the Spirit tore a streetlamp from the ground to use as a lantern. They soon were on their way.

Shortly, the Spirit and Scrooge arrived at a tiny run-down house.

"What a dreadful little house," Scrooge exclaimed, looking in the window. "Who could live in such a place? Perhaps a miserable beggar?"

"Look closer, Scrooge," advised the Spirit, "and tell me who you see."

Scrooge pressed his face against the glass for a better look.

"Why, it's Bob Cratchit, my clerk!" he said with surprise. "Does he live *here*?"

The Spirit scowled. "Look at how he lives, thanks to your 'generosity'. Look at the food his family must eat this Christmas Eve, because it's all they can afford."

The hungry Cratchit family sat at their table, about to carve up the smallest goose Scrooge had ever seen in his life.

"Surely they have more food than that." Scrooge said. "Look on the fire.

"That's your laundry!" the Spirit said.

Scrooge was ashamed. As he watched, a boy named Tiny Tim hobbled into the room, leaning on a little crutch. He gave thanks to Scrooge for their meal.

"Tell me, Spirit, what's wrong with that kind lad?" Scrooge asked.

"Much, I'm afraid," the Spirit replied. "If these shadows remain unchanged, I see an empty chair where Tiny Tim once sat."

Suddenly, the scene went dark. When Scrooge stepped back from the window, the Spirit had disappeared. Only two giant footprints indicated that he had been there at all. In the distance, church bells tolled.

"Don't go!" Scrooge cried. "You must tell me about Tim! Don't go."

Just then, the swirling smoke grew thicker and thicker until Scrooge could not see anything around him. The smoke blew into his nose, and he coughed.

As the smoke lifted, Scrooge looked around. He was standing in a graveyard! There were tombstones everywhere, covered by a layer of snow.

Scrooge looked up. He was no longer alone. A horrible shadow, his face hidden inside his cloak, stood silently before him.

"A-are you the Ghost of Christmas Future?"

Scrooge stammered.

"Tell me, what will happen to Tiny Tim?"

The Spirit looked at Scrooge silently and raised his large arm.

Scrooge looked to where the Spirit was pointing into
the distance. He saw Bob Cratchit and his family
gathered around a tombstone.

They were all crying.

Bob Cratchit knelt before the little gravestone. Gently, he laid Tiny Tim's crutch on the grave, tears rolling down his face.

"Oh, no," Scrooge cried.

"Spirit, I didn't want this to happen. Tell me that these events can yet be changed!"

Suddenly, the church bells tolled again. Scrooge noticed two gravediggers finishing a fresh grave.

"I've never seen a funeral like this one,"

the first one said.

"No mourners, no friends to bid him farewell," the second one chimed in.

"Oh, well," the first one added. "Let's rest a minute before we fill it in, eh?"

"He ain't going nowhere,"

the second replied as they both walked off, laughing.

Scrooge peered down into the grave. "Spirit, whose lonely grave is this?" he asked.

"Why, it's *yours*, Ebenezer!" the Spirit laughed as his hood fell from his face.

"The richest man in the cemetery," the Spirit cackled as he pushed Scrooge into the grave. It burst into flames!

"No, no, no!" Scrooge cried.

"I'll change!"

"Let me out!" Scrooge screamed. "Let me—"

Suddenly, another bell tolled. Scrooge opened his eyes and shouted with joy. He was in his room!

Scrooge jumped up and ran to the window. The sun shone brightly, and the church bells were ringing.

"It's Christmas morning!"

Scrooge cried.

"I haven't missed it. The spirits have given me another chance. I know just what I'll do! They'll be so surprised. There's so much to do!"

Throwing on his coat and hat, Scrooge raced out the door.

As Scrooge ran down the road, he saw his nephew, Fred, approaching in a wagon.

"I'm looking forward to that wonderful meal of yours,"

Scrooge said merrily.

"You're coming?"

Fred asked in disbelief.

"Of course I am!" Scrooge replied.

Fred was so surprised by his uncle's cheerfulness that he almost fell off his carriage. Waving goodbye to his nephew, Scrooge continued on his way.

Rat! Tat!

Bob Cratchit heard a sharp knock and opened his door. His face fell when he saw who was standing on the step. It was Scrooge, holding a big brown sack on his back. He looked very angry.

"Why, Mr. Scrooge, Merry Christmas. Won't you come in?"

Scrooge stomped into the living room.

"Merry Christmas, ha! I have another bundle for you,"

Scrooge said, dropping the heavy bag to the floor.

"B-but sir, it's Christmas Day," Cratchit stammered.

"Christmas Day, indeed. Just another excuse for being lazy!" Scrooge scowled. "And another thing, Cratchit. I've had enough of this 'day off' stuff. You leave me no alternative but to give you . . ."

"Toys!" Tiny Tim shouted, pulling open the bag. Parcels tied with bright ribbons and bows tumbled from the sack. Scrooge laughed as the children's faces lit up with joy.

Scrooge smiled at Cratchit.

"I'm giving you a raise. And making you my partner."

Cratchit couldn't believe it. "Oh, thank you, Mr. Scrooge!"

"Merry Christmas, Bob," Scrooge said as the whole family danced with joy. It was a Christmas miracle.

"And God bless us, every one," said Tiny Tim.

"The spirit of Christmas is love, you know."

—Donald Duck

DONALD DUCK'S
CHRISTMAS TREE

IT WAS THE DAY BEFORE

Christmas. Inside Donald Duck's house, all the stockings were hung carefully by the chimney. He had wrapped all the presents for his nephews, Huey, Dewey, and Louie.

Donald had just finished icing a hot batch of gingerbread cookies. They were shaped like snowmen, bells, stars, and Christmas trees. Then Donald remembered something.

He still needed to get a *real* Christmas tree.

Donald put on his coat, cap, and mittens. Then he picked up his sharp, shiny ax. He wanted to cut down the best Christmas tree for his nephews.

"Come along, Pluto," he called.

"We're going to the woods
to find our Christmas tree."

Pluto came running through the heavy blanket of
snow. Together, they went into the snowy forest.

Meanwhile, deep in the woods in a sturdy fir tree lived two merry chipmunks named Chip and Dale.

They were also getting ready for Christmas. They had found a tiny sapling standing in the snow near their home. They were trimming the tree with berries and dry grass when they heard a noise.

The chipmunks heard Donald whistling through the woods. Then they saw Pluto prancing at his side.

They dropped their decorations and scampered to safety atop their snowy fir tree home.

At least, they *thought* they were safe.

But what was this? While Pluto sniffed around in the snow, Donald circled the sturdy fir tree. He looked it over for a minute and then turned to Pluto.

"This is just the tree for us,"
Donald said.

Pluto barked in agreement.

Donald went to work with his sharp, shiny ax.

Chop, chop,
        chop, chop,
                chop, chop!

Poor Chip and Dale, hidden in the treetop, were too scared to move.

"TIMBERRRR!" Donald cried as the tree came crashing down. Chip and Dale clung on for dear life.

"Come on, Pluto," Donald called. "Let's take our tree home."

So Donald and Pluto headed home, Donald whistling as they went, dragging the fir tree behind them.

And up in the branches Chip and Dale sat quietly, enjoying the nice ride.

Back at home, Donald set up the tree in his living room.

"There," he said as he adjusted it.
"Now to trim the tree."

Donald raced to his closet and pulled out two large boxes of ornaments and garlands.

From their hiding places up in the branches, Chip and Dale looked on curiously.

The two chipmunks watched as Donald looped long strings of colorful bulbs over the branches of the tree. Donald wove his way around the tree until it was completely covered in multicolored lights.

Then Donald began hanging brightly colored gold, red, and blue balls on the branches of the tree. Pluto helped him where he could.

Pluto gave Donald the last of the ornaments. Donald stood back to admire their work. "Doesn't that look great?" he asked. Pluto wagged his tail in agreement.

It was indeed a beautiful Christmas tree.

"Now I'll pile the presents underneath for Mickey, Minnie, Huey, Dewey, and Louie, and Daisy," Donald said. "You stay here, Pluto. I'll be right back."

As Donald went to grab the presents, Pluto admired the glowing Christmas tree. He loved looking at all the ornaments and lights.

Up in the tree, Chip and Dale watched as Donald disappeared from sight. They were excited by the beautiful lights and ornaments in their tree. Looking at each other, they danced on the branches until the needles shook.

They made faces at themselves in the shiny colored balls. Their warped reflections made them laugh until their little sides shook.

Pluto noticed the two chipmunks in the tree.

He growled disapprovingly.

But Chip and Dale didn't care.

Chip just picked a shiny blue ball off the tree and threw it at the dog!

Pluto caught it in his paw.

The mischievous chipmunks began throwing more ornaments at him!

Pluto jumped up and started catching the ornaments in his paws and teeth.

Just then,
Donald came back in.

"Pluto!" he cried.
"Bad dog!"

He thought Pluto had been snatching ornaments from the tree!

Poor Pluto! He barked at the tree and sniffed at the branches. But the two chipmunks had disappeared!

"Now be good while I bring in the rest of the presents,"

Donald said as he placed the presents under the tree and walked out of the room again.

No sooner had he left than Chip and Dale appeared!

They danced down the branches, playing with the lights.

Plunk! Chip's head went through a colored ball. Dale laughed as Chip danced around the branches with a big round golden head.

But Pluto didn't think it was funny at all. They were going to ruin Donald's Christmas tree!

He growled at the chipmunks.

But they wouldn't stop messing around. Pluto leaned back, ready to jump.

"Pluto!" Donald cried. "What is the matter with you? Do you want to ruin the tree?"

Pluto spun around to look at the tree again.
But Chip and Dale were out of sight!

Poor Pluto couldn't explain.

"I can't have you ruining the tree," Donald said.
"I guess you'll have to go out to your doghouse for the
rest of Christmas Eve."

Pluto howled sadly. Just then, Chip grew tired of
wearing his round golden mask. He pulled off the ball
and let it drop.

Crash! It fell to the floor.

"What was that?"

Donald cried.

Pluto barked, looking toward the tree. Dale was hidden in the tree, playing with the colored lights, twisting them so they turned off and on.

"What's this?" Donald cried.

Pluto barked again. Donald peered through the branches until he spied Chip and Dale.

"Well, well,"

he chuckled, lifting the two chipmunks down.

"So you're the ones who have been making mischief. I'm sorry I blamed you, Pluto."

Pluto marched angrily to the front door and held it open. He thought Chip and Dale should go out in the snow!

"Oh, Pluto," Donald said. "It's Christmas Eve. We must be kind to everyone. The spirit of Christmas is love, you know."

So Pluto made friends with Chip and Dale, and they apologized to him. And when Huey, Dewey, and Louie came over, they all agreed that this was by far the happiest Christmas Eve they could remember.

"She's worth her weight in gold."

—*Mickey Mouse*

MICKEY AND MINNIE'S
GIFT _{OF} _{THE} MAGI

─── ★ ───

IT WAS THE DAY BEFORE

Christmas. The bright morning sun was sparkling on the freshly fallen snow. There was a chill in the air as Mickey and Pluto strolled down the street.

Mickey's coat was old and tattered. His Christmas tree was small. And his pockets were as empty as the stockings hanging in homes all over town, waiting to be filled. But Mickey was happy.

Suddenly, Pluto started to bark. He pulled Mickey over to a shop window. Inside was a beautiful golden chain that twinkled in the morning sunlight.

"That's it, Pluto," Mickey sighed. "The perfect gift to go with Minnie's watch."

Mickey reached into his pockets. "I'm a little short right now," he told Pluto. "But we're going to make lots of tips today, aren't we?"

Pluto looked doubtfully at Mickey.

"Come on," Mickey said. "Let's get this tree to Minnie's. We'll come back for the chain later."

Meanwhile, at home, Minnie was worrying over a pile of unpaid bills. "Oh, Figaro," she sighed, "how am I ever going to afford to buy Mickey a present?"

Just then, Minnie heard a knock at the door.

She quickly shoved the bills in a drawer and raced into the living room.

Minnie opened the front door to find Mickey carrying a tree and playing a happy song on his harmonica.

Minnie giggled. "Oh, Mickey, when you play the harmonica, my heart sings."

Mickey brought the tree inside. Then he wrapped his harmonica in an old rag.

"You know, an instrument like that deserves a special case," Minnie told him.

"I suppose it does," Mickey said. "Maybe someday it will have one."

Mickey asked Minnie what time it was.

"Let's see," Minnie replied, pulling a string out of her pocket. On the end hung a lovely old watch.

"I bet that would look real nice on a gold chain," Mickey said.

Minnie took another look at her watch.

"Oh, my goodness!
        I'm late for work!"

she exclaimed.

Minnie quickly put her watch away and headed for the door. But Mickey beat her outside. He and Pluto wanted to drop her off—in style!

Pluto pulled up in front of Mortimer's Department Store. Minnie had made it to work just in time!

Minnie gave Mickey a quick kiss and then dashed inside.

Mickey turned to Pluto.

"Come on, fella, we have work to do!"

Together, the pair hurried off.

Unfortunately, dropping Minnie off had made Mickey late for his own job at Crazy Pete's Christmas Tree Farm.

"Merry Christmas, Mr. Pete," Mickey said when he arrived.

"I'll be merry when I've sold all those ten-footers!" Pete barked.

"Now get to work!"

The day was busier than Mickey had expected. It seemed that many people had waited till the last minute to buy their trees. Even better, the customers were so impressed with Mickey's help that he earned a lot of extra money.

"Hot dog!" Mickey exclaimed. "Looks like we'll be able to get Minnie that chain for her watch after all!"

Nearby, Pete was trying to convince a poor family to buy an expensive Christmas tree.

"That's all I've got left," Pete lied.

"You don't want these kids going without a tree now, do ya?"

Over on his side of the lot, Mickey heard Pete. He didn't think his boss was being fair. "How about this smaller tree?" Mickey called out. "I found it in the back!"

The children were delighted. "It's perfect!"

"We'll take it!" their father said. "Thank you! And Merry Christmas!"

After the family left, Pete was furious. "I had them on the hook for a ten-foot tree!" he growled at Mickey. "I'm taking what I would have made off that tree out of *your* pay!"

And with that, Pete snatched Mickey's money right out of his hand.

"Now get out of my sight!" Pete roared, tossing Mickey and Pluto headfirst into the snow.

"You're fired!"

Across town at Mortimer's, Minnie was busy wrapping Christmas gifts.

"I really want to get Mickey something special this year," Minnie told her friend Daisy. "But I can't do it without that Christmas bonus!"

Just then, the phone rang. It was Minnie's boss. He wanted to see her in his office.

Minnie put down the gift she was wrapping and raced upstairs.

Minnie was sure she was about to get her Christmas bonus. But when she reached her boss's office, Mr. Mortimer handed her a gift instead.

"A fruitcake?" Minnie said, surprised. She tried to hide her disappointment. "Thank you, sir."

"No need to thank me,"

Mr. Mortimer replied.

Minnie left his office. "How am I ever going to get Mickey a present now?" she sighed sadly.

Meanwhile, Mickey sat in the park playing his harmonica. He had lost his job *and* his money. How could he pay for Minnie's present now?

Then the fire chief heard Mickey playing. The local firemen were putting on a concert to collect Christmas toys for orphans, and they needed a harmonica player!

Mickey happily agreed to play for them.

Soon his music was delighting everyone. The listeners were so moved that they donated lots of toys!

"You and that harmonica make a great team," the fire chief told Mickey when the concert was over.

"She's worth her weight in gold," Mickey agreed.

His eyes lit up. "That's it!"
he shouted. "Come on, Pluto!
We still have time to get to the
shop before it closes."

The pair borrowed a snowboard and flew through the streets. They made it to the shop just as the shopkeeper was locking the door.

Mickey begged the shopkeeper to reopen the store, but the owner just shook his head. He needed to get home to his family.

Mickey sat on the curb and played his harmonica sadly. Touched by Mickey's beautiful Christmas song, the shopkeeper changed his mind about closing his shop. He unlocked the door and let Mickey trade his harmonica for the gold chain in the window.

Later that night, Mickey and Minnie sat in front of the fire with Pluto and Figaro, preparing to exchange gifts. Mickey handed Minnie a beautifully wrapped box.

"I hope you like it!"

he told her.

Minnie unwrapped her gift first.

"A chain for my watch!"
she exclaimed.

"Oh, Mickey, it's beautiful. I love it! But I traded in my watch to buy your gift. . . ."

Mickey slowly unwrapped his gift.

"A case for my harmonica,"
he said.

Mickey looked at Minnie. "I traded my harmonica to get the chain for your watch," he confessed.

"Oh, Mickey, I can't believe you gave up what means the most to you for *me*!" Minnie exclaimed.

"Minnie, don't you know you're all the music I'll ever need?"

Mickey asked.

"Merry Christmas, Mickey!" Minnie said happily.

Mickey took her hand. "Merry Christmas, Minnie."

The couple smiled at each other. It was a Christmas they'd never forget!

"If we tried real hard it might help."

—*Huey Duck*

HUEY, DEWEY, AND LOUIE'S
CHRISTMAS WISH

I T WAS A FEW DAYS BEFORE Christmas, and the town was buzzing with excitement. Three brothers, Huey, Dewey, and Louie, were walking along the snow-covered streets, looking eagerly in the windows of the storefronts.

"Wow, look at that shiny toboggan!" Dewey cried. He pulled his two brothers over to a brightly lit window.

"We sure could have a lot of fun with that if we got it for Christmas," sighed Huey.

"But we've already mailed our letter to Santa, so it's too late to ask him," Louie pointed out.

"We could ask Uncle Donald,"

Dewey suggested.

"But we haven't *exactly* been the most well-behaved boys in the world."

"Well, if we tried real hard it might help," Huey said.

"Sure! We could shovel the walk—" Louie began.

"Make our beds—" Dewey continued.

"And even wash the dishes," Huey finished.

"Come on! Let's get started!" Louie cried. "Uncle Donald will be looking for Daisy's Christmas present tomorrow. Maybe we can get him past this window."

"We're right behind you!"

Huey and Dewey yelled as they raced for home.

Later that day, Donald was amazed when he looked out the window and saw his three nephews shoveling the walk.

After supper, he was even more astonished to see them clear the table and do the dishes.

In the evening, the boys sat quietly and read their storybooks.

Donald was confused! Normally the boys were rowdy and loud.

"They're either sick or planning some mischief,"

Donald said to himself.

He shook his head as he watched Huey, Dewey, and Louie troop up the stairs to bed at nine o'clock.

A little while later, Donald padded softly up the stairs. He poked his head into the boys' room. "This is too good to be true!" he whispered to himself. The three boys were sleeping peacefully.

The next morning, Donald went to wake the boys. But their beds were neatly made, and they were nowhere in sight!

He hurried down the steps.
Where could they be?
As he walked into the
kitchen, he spotted them.
They were waiting for
him. Breakfast was already
on the table!

After breakfast, Donald put on his coat to head in to town.

"Could we please go downtown with you today, Uncle Donald?" Dewey asked.

"Well, I guess so, since you three have been behaving," Donald answered.

The boys chatted merrily all the way downtown. Before Donald even realized what was happening, they had steered him down the street directly toward a certain store.

"Uncle Donald, did you ever go tobogganing when you were small?" Huey asked.

"Why, I almost grew up on the slopes tobogganing,"

Donald answered.

"Really? Was it fun, Uncle Donald?" Louie asked.

Now they were in front of the store window.

"It was great sport, and—" Donald started to say.

"Look at that swell toboggan, Uncle Donald!" the three boys cried at once.

"Ah-ha! So that's it!"

Donald squawked.

"No wonder you've been behaving. You want me to get you that toboggan for Christmas. Well, that's out! Look at the price!"

And with that, he shooed them past the store and down the street.

As they neared home, Donald started feeling a little sorry for the boys.

"Now, boys," he told them, "your sled is still in good shape. You can have lots of fun with that."

Daisy

Slowly, the three brothers walked over to where their old sled leaned against a tree.

"Okay, Uncle Donald, but a toboggan would sure be nice," they said sadly.

That night, as soon as the boys had gone to bed, Donald hurried downstairs. He hoped the store would be open. He felt bad that he had been so hard on the boys, and he wanted to buy them the toboggan as a Christmas surprise.

The store was open, but the toboggan was gone!

When Donald asked about it, the sales clerk told him that it had been sold—and that it had been the last one in town.

Donald felt miserable as he trudged home. "Now what will I do?" he asked himself. "The boys didn't ask Santa for a toboggan, and I can't find one for them anywhere!"

The next morning, Huey, Dewey, and Louie raced downtown for another look at the toboggan.

When they arrived at the storefront, the toboggan was no longer in the window. In its place was a shiny wagon.

"Hooray for Uncle Donald!"

they shouted.

"He got it for us. Now we *have* to keep on being good."

But Donald hadn't found a toboggan for them, even though he had looked everywhere. He had gone to Hall's Hardware. He had tried Davis's Dry Goods. He had even looked at Drew's Drugstore.

On Christmas Eve, Donald tossed and turned in his sleep, dreaming of toboggans.

On Christmas morning, Donald jerked upright in bed. He could hear Huey, Dewey, and Louie shouting excitedly. He hurried downstairs.

When Donald reached the living room, he saw the
boys staring out the window.

"Look, Uncle Donald!"

they shouted.

Outside on the snow was a beautiful toboggan. Strange little hoofprints led away from it, and written in large letters in the snow was a message.

Huey, Dewey, and Louie jumped up and down excitedly. Donald smiled and hugged his nephews. Santa had seen what good boys they'd been and left them a special present.

Together, they all ran outside to go for a Christmas morning ride.

Collection copyright © 2017 Disney Enterprises, Inc.

Individual copyrights and permissions for works included in this collection:

"Mickey's Christmas Carol" adapted from the book written by Disney Book Group
and illustrated by the Disney Storybook Art Team.
Copyright © 2012 Disney Enterprises, Inc.

"Donald Duck's Christmas Tree" adapted from the book *Walt Disney's Donald Duck's Christmas Tree*
written by Annie North Bedford. Illustrations adapted by Bob Moore.
Copyright © 1954, 2006 Disney Enterprises, Inc.

"Mickey and Minnie's Gift of the Magi" based on the story by Bruce Talkington and illustrated by Fernando Guell Cano.
Copyright © 2001, 2012 Disney Enterprises, Inc.

"Huey, Dewey, and Louie's Christmas Wish" adapted from the book *Walt Disney's Donald Duck: Huey, Louie,
and Dewey's Christmas Wish* by Mary L. Hilt and illustrated by Nathalee Mode and James Fletcher.
Copyright © 1962 Walt Disney Productions.

All rights reserved. Published by Disney Press, an imprint of Disney Book Group.
No part of this book may be reproduced or transmitted in any form or by any means, electronic or
mechanical, including photocopying, recording, or by any information storage and retrieval system,
without written permission from the publisher.

For information address Disney Press, 1101 Flower Street, Glendale, California 91201.

Printed in the United States of America

First Hardcover Edition, September 2017

Library of Congress Control Number: 2016948948

3 5 7 9 10 8 6 4 2

ISBN 978-1-368-00256-1

FAC-038091-18201

For more Disney Press fun, visit www.disneybooks.com